a radiant curve

VOLUME 64

Sun Tracks

An American Indian Literary Series

THE UNIVERSITY OF ARIZONA PRESS | TUCSON

a radiant curve
LUCI TAPAHONSO

poems and stories

The University of Arizona Press

© 2008 Luci Tapahonso

Library of Congress Cataloging-in-
Publication data appear on the last
printed page of this book.

Publication of this book is made
possible in part by the proceeds of a
permanent endowment created with
the assistance of a Challenge Grant
from the National Endowment for
the Humanities, a federal agency.

Manufactured in the United States
of America on acid-free, archival-
quality paper containing a minimum
of 30% post-consumer waste and
processed chlorine free.

13 12 11 10 09 08   6 5 4 3 2 1

For our youngest grandchildren:

Nihisóóké Christian Michael Melendez,

dóó Isaiah Tsétah James,

dóó Samiyah Deezbaa' James,

dóó Nihináliké Tatum Elizabeth Martin,

dóó Derek Robert Martin.

Háshinee'. 'Ayóó 'ádanihíínish'ní.

contents

a radiant curve

The beginning was mist.
The first Holy Ones talked and sang as always.
They created light, night, and day.
They sang into place the mountains,
the rivers, plants, and animals.
They sang us into life.

The warp is even: taut vertical loops

between our father and the earth.
Today I began anew:
in the gray pre-dawn the air is moist.
As I walk, my footsteps echo in the still morning;
damp, fragrant circles appeared overnight on the cold driveway.
Soon they will vanish with the sun's first rays,
but now I breathe the sweet dampness.
Suddenly I miss my father so.
How he savored such mornings.
He would have spoken to the solitary dove
that sits on the edge of the red tile roof.
Its long, delicate coos are the rhythmic pauses of desert mornings.

Today I began anew.
This afternoon, after phone calls and class preparations,
I sit in the bright sunlight and twist, then loop
the dark edging cords along the top and bottom of the loom.
My fingers move easily between the turns of yarn: such needed slants of rain.
"It hasn't rained here for months," I tell the loom.
On a clear, quiet afternoon last spring, my mother said,
"It's hard to see now; my eyes are getting weak."
It seemed that she had been thinking of this for some time.

Today, the tightly spun dark red yarn falls into place evenly.
I began anew for my mother, and some things
she remembers as she looks at rugs:

3

The long afternoons decades ago when the children slept,
the soft tamping of her batten comb echoed in the small house.
The intricate double-sided rugs her mother-in-law wove.
Even now, 70 years later, she marvels at the saddle rug
Nihinálí 'Ásdzą́ą́n made for her husband, my father.
I began anew for my mother's memories.

Today, I began anew.
On the mantel is the small basketball my grandson left when he last visited.
I look down the bright hallway and recall his bubbling baby laughter.
His dark, shiny eyes glitter with delight.
I easily recall the warm tautness of his little body in my arms.
His black, thick hair against the bend of my elbow.
He lets me carry him as if he were an infant.
I sing old songs, and he watches me.
He watches the huge blue sky overhead.
I sing songs created for him, "Whose little boy are you?
Said I am grandma's boy. Grandma's little baby boy."
As he listens intently to the songs
and watches the skies of his homeland,
I memorize everything.

I wish for such moments every day.
I weave the first four rows of black yarn
for my little grandson, who inherited my father's name:
Hastiin Tsétah Naaki Bísóí.

The warp is even: taut vertical loops
between our father and the earth.

The Holy People lived here in the beginning.
They built the first hooghan, made the first weapons,
sang the first songs and made the first prayers.
Diné language, ceremonies,
history, and beliefs began here.
This is where we began.

A Radiant Curve

One fall afternoon in 1998, my daughter Misty called to tell us that her infant son Isaiah had just laughed aloud. It was anticipated, because when a Diné, or Navajo, baby laughs aloud for the first time, a First Laugh ceremony is usually held. Shisóí Isaiah (*Shisóí* means "my daughter's child") had laughed in his sleep, and as a baby he still lived in the world of the Diyin Dine'é, or the Holy People. But this time he had been awake when his father, Lloyd James, tickled him. This occurrence showed that Shisóí had consciously performed the act of thinking, Ntsékees, which is associated with the beginning of creation, childhood, and the sunrise.

Centuries ago, the Holy People decreed that Diné children be honored in this fashion, because before this first genuine expression of emotion, the infant still "belonged to" and lived in the world of the Holy People. The first laugh marks the first step of his or her moving away from this sphere and the beginning of the child's participation in the human family's network. The next step occurs when the child speaks his or her first words.

There was excitement, as the First Laugh ceremony would be held within four days of the first laugh. Since Lloyd had made Isaiah laugh, he would normally be obligated to host the dinner, but Lloyd and Misty lived in an apartment, so the ceremony and dinner would be held at our house, which could accommodate people comfortably. Our other grandchildren were giddy with delight; they, too, had the ceremony when they were infants, and now they would play important roles in the preparations. The house was filled with laughter and cheer as we began to plan and to issue invitations via phone and notes on friends' doors.

This ceremony, rich with time, was first performed for White Shell Girl, who grew to become Changing Woman, a principal deity who created the ancestors of the present-day Diné. Today the Navajo Nation encompasses 25,000 square miles in the states of Utah, New Mexico, and Arizona. Near the center of this land is Dinétah, where the Diyin Dine'é, the Holy People, resided after their emergence into the present world. The current population of the Diné is estimated to be 300,000. Over time, many people left the Navajo country for various reasons: kidnappings by the Spanish and other intruders, forced removal by the government, escape from enemies, and the compulsory mandates of the boarding schools in the 1800s. Later, off-reservation boarding schools, the military draft, and government relocation programs became the major basis for the continuing displacements. The change from the traditional Diné lifestyle to a wage economy in the mid-1900s also caused many people to seek employment away from the Navajo homeland.

In spite of these departures, which were often involuntary, many of the venerable and essential tenets that Changing Woman and the Diyin Dine'é outlined at the beginning of Navajo time have endured. Each time various rituals are performed, specific stories, songs, and prayers accompany them. The First Laugh and the Kinaałdá, a coming-of-age ceremony for Navajo girls, are part of the Beauty Way, or Hózhǫ́ǫ́jí, ceremonies.

At the time of Isaiah's first laugh, my husband, Robert Martin, was president of Haskell Indian Nations University, and I was teaching at the University of Kansas in Lawrence. Two of our daughters and their children lived in Lawrence also, but we consider our "real home" to be Navajo country. My family and extended family live in and around Shiprock, New Mexico, where we make pilgrimages several times a year.

My daughters and I communicated via cell phones and e-mail as we, and at times our husbands, prepared food for the approximately forty people that would attend the ceremony. That evening everything was ready except for the mutton stew and bread, which would be made in the morning. Various dishes of mutton or lamb were prepared as important symbols of sustenance, prosperity, and kinship.

Meanwhile, the children were noisily occupied with making gift bundles of shiny cellophane packages fastened with ribbon. They assumed this "job" because as children, they "just knew" what their little brother Isaiah wanted to give as gifts. (In Diné families, the children of one's aunts and uncles are considered siblings, rather than cousins.) The bundles contained bubble gum, packages of animal crackers, lollipops, tiny plastic cars, and other treats and toys. As the children assembled the gifts, they talked about Changing Woman's upcoming visit to our home, as well as the wishes they would request of Isaiah in his role as Changing Woman.

The men brought bags of oranges, apples, bananas, and other fruit. These were placed in large baskets to be given along with the gift bundles. They rearranged the rooms to provide enough seating, and a section of the west side of the living room was prepared where Isaiah would sit with his parents. They draped Pendleton shawls over the couches and chairs, and cleared a space for the baskets, which would be placed along the east wall. It is said that the Holy People arrive daily at sunrise from the east, and this is reinforced in prayers, songs, and ceremonies indicating that all of creation began in the east.

That evening as we gathered for dinner, we reviewed details, then my husband suggested that I tell the story of the First Laugh ceremony. So we settled in for a session of hané. This story, like many others that guide Diné life today, can be traced back to 'Áłk'idą́ą́, "Long Ago," or the beginning of Diné time. *Hané* means "stories" and implies a sense of history (hence "'Áłk'idą́ą́"), but also serves as a signal to pay attention. In order for one to grasp the meaning of the story, his or her mental and emotional participation are necessary. Even though 'Áłk'idą́ą́ means "long ago" or "of an ancient time," in such stories the literal date is not questioned, because it is understood that aspects of "'Áłk'idą́ą́ hané" are connected to the time when Diné concepts were being formed. Thus children can understand how events that occurred many centuries ago are important in their own daily lives. They will quiet down for a story, as all children will, but they also know that because they are Diné and from specific clans, 'Áłk'idą́ą́ hané can teach them new things about who they are. The story begins with "'Áłk'idą́ą́ jiní," which means "long ago they said."

'Áłk'idą́ą́ jiní, long ago they said, Áłtsé 'Asdzą́ą́n, First Woman, and Áłtsé Hastiin, First Man, called upon 'Áshįįh 'Asdzą́ą́n Sání, Old Salt Woman, to come to Dził Ná'oodiłii, or Huerfano Mesa, where they lived. On this day, Old Salt Woman was called because First Woman and First Man's baby, White Shell Girl, was listless and unhappy. White Shell Girl was the first Diné child, and her parents, as well as the other Holy People, were very mindful of their sacred responsibilities. White Shell Girl would grow up to become a primary deity, Changing Woman.

White Shell Girl was found on a small hill (Gobernador Knob) by First Man, who was guided by her infant cries, as well as the unusual sight of a dark cloud atop the hill on an otherwise clear day. After offering specific songs and prayers, he brought her home to First Woman. White Shell Girl was wrapped in a cloud beneath a rainbow drenched in dewdrops, and they said that with each breath she took, "the dawn lifted." Thus white symbolizes birth or the beginning of life, because "everything came to life" when First Man found White Shell Girl. First Man's songs and prayers as he neared the baby are now the components of a Blessing Way ceremony to ensure a safe and healthy childbirth.

As time passed, Changing Woman raised her sons, the Twin Warriors, on Huerfano Mesa. They, too, played crucial roles in the development of Diné history and beliefs. Regardless of where the ceremonies they gave us are held, it is a way to invite the Holy People into our homes and let them know that we strive to be good parents and good relatives as they wished. It is said that the Diyin Dine'é, the Holy People, appear at dawn each morning. After they set the world in place for us, they retreated to live within the sacred mountains: Sisnaajinii (Blanca Peak), Tsoodził (Mount Taylor), Dook'ooosłííd (San Francisco Peaks), and Dibé Ntsaa (La Plata Mountains). They did not abandon us; they return each morning to "check on us." Thus we are told to go outside and pray with corn pollen facing the sunrise. "Get up early and go pray," parents and grandparents say, "so that you can get your blessings. Otherwise, you'll grow up to be lazy and poor."

Today, Diné far away from the sight of the sacred mountains can be comforted by praying at dawn, no matter where they are, and the Diyin Dine'é acknowledge them because they are within the light of dawn.

Old Salt Woman was known for her cheerful and generous nature. Once she had lived at Dinétah, but it had become crowded, so she moved near present-day Fence Lake, New Mexico, which is a considerable distance away. They say that as she walked from her home across the many miles to Dził Ná'oodiłii, or Huerfano Mesa, she created baby songs and lullabies, which included gestures, imitations of animals and birds, and other unique expressions. Thus we know that lullabies, children's songs, and traveling songs existed early on. The Holy People gave much thought to how children would be raised: their physical and emotional growth, as well as the ways to speak to a child.

Meanwhile, there was quite a gathering at White Shell Girl's hooghan; many people and animals had arrived. At this time all beings were able to communicate freely and easily. Much food had been prepared, and gifts of various crops, fruit, herbs, and miniature replicas of animals and household utensils were spread on a blanket. First Woman and First Man bestowed gifts on others to honor Old Salt Woman's generosity.

They heard Old Salt Woman singing as she approached from a distance; an aura of happiness and gaiety preceded her. She wore a dress of crystalline grains of salt and seemed to glow with cheerfulness. She stepped into the hooghan, and after formal greetings, she approached White Shell Girl and cradled her carefully. Her voice rose and fell in lilting, rhythmic songs as she rocked and swayed with White Shell Girl. Then Old Salt Woman paused at the east side of the hooghan and tickled the baby's chin, saying, "Wooshíí, wooshíí." This word, meaning "tickle," brings a smile to everyone. Then she put a grain of salt into White Shell Girl's mouth, who laughed aloud — her bright laughter filling the hooghan. Such a radiant sound had never been heard before.

Everyone was overjoyed as the baby beamed with happiness. Old Salt Woman helped White Shell Girl hand salt to all those who were present. Old Salt Woman instructed them to ask for blessings, because the baby was a holy being who could grant such wishes. White Shell Girl then gave out herbs, fresh corn, and small clay toys as gifts, thus ensuring she would grow to be a generous person.

The hooghan was filled with much laughter, songs, and stories as food was served. As White Shell Girl giggled, kicking and waving her arms about, the First Laugh dinner was born: a celebration that ensures the baby's happiness and emphasizes the import of a sense of humor.

Many relatives and friends are invited so that the baby will never experience loneliness and will always be surrounded by the love and concern of many. The Holy People wanted to ensure that the baby would be aware of her extended family and the larger Diné community.

The ceremony also honors Old Salt Woman, because she taught that one needs 'áshįįh, salt, to remain strong and healthy. In fact, medicine man Raymond Jim Redhouse, who specializes in the Wind Way and Blessing Way ceremonies, teaches that we need nine types of salt to exist. Old Salt Woman is a role model of Diné ideals: remaining physically healthy, maintaining a positive attitude, and attaining old age.

Sometimes it is suggested that a person who is sullen be given a dose of salt; this makes members of the Salt Clan happy. But it is also said that the 'Áshįįhí are naturally good-natured and generous — a tribute to 'Áshįįh 'Asdzą́ą́n Sání, as she is the progenitor of the Salt Clan.

The various beings and Diyin Dine'é took part in White Shell Girl's upbringing. She was taught songs and prayers about every facet of daily life: cooking songs, weaving songs, songs to keep animals healthy, songs for fixing one's hair, hooghan songs, songs for birds and other creatures, and planting songs. Parents are complimented when someone says, "Your children are well-behaved and respectful; you must really talk to them." In "talking to" a child, our traditional beliefs are passed on in a respectful and spiritual way, as this was how White Shell Girl was treated.

When we listen to 'Átk'idą́ą́ hané, stories from the beginning of Diné time, we respect and continue to adhere to the Holy People's teachings. They laid out a diagram of life for us, the Diné, to follow, and no matter where we live or what path we undertake, their teachings always guide us.

The hané concluded that evening: the second day after Shisóí Isaiah laughed. Our children and grandchildren got up to leave, and they checked things one more time in the living room. They had corn pollen for prayers at dawn.

After they left and the house became quiet, joyful expectation lingered in the air. I whispered a prayer of gratitude for the gift baskets, the huge bowls of fruit, the rearranged room, the blanket-draped furniture, and the many containers of prepared food. I recalled the First Laugh Ceremonies of my children, then my grandchildren, and the ways they embodied, perhaps without realizing it, the many qualities that Changing Woman/Old Salt Woman and the Holy People hoped to instill: respect, sharing, and appreciation of family and kin. This must have been how First Woman and First Man felt, I thought, as they prepared for Old Salt Woman's arrival. They were thankful and happy, and they believed in what the future held for them and their descendents.

Early the next morning, though the sun was obscured by thick mist, I offered prayers on the front porch. When we looked for a home in Lawrence, I told the realtor that a major consideration was that the front door face east. In each home we have lived, this has been the case. Though we live away from Dinétah, this is one way to maintain the traditions regarding the hooghan, the home.

This concept of the east and sunrise relates to the day when First Man found the baby who was a "white shell held by glistening mist," and when the Diyin Dine'é created Blanca Peak and the other sacred mountains. All prayers and songs begin with references to Blanca Peak and White Shell Girl, among other aspects, and so one enters a ceremonial hooghan from the east and proceeds in a clockwise pattern. So the "proper way" to begin any task or project is to start in the east, then south, then west, and finally, north. This idea can be applied to cleaning a home, stirring a pot of food, leading a discussion, developing a project, or in this case, preparing for a First Laugh dinner.

On the day of the ceremony, as Misty and Lloyd greeted people, the grandchildren took turns offering coffee, water, or soft drinks. Shisóí Isaiah was very observant and curious about the attention directed at him. We had arranged the ceremony in the afternoon after his usual nap, so he would be alert. He shook hands politely with everyone when his parents said, "Yá'át'ééh diní" (shake hands "hello"). Though he didn't smile readily at the guests, he had an open and thoughtful expression.

After the meal, we gathered in the living room. Since some guests were not Diné, I spoke about the significance of Shisóí Isaiah entering a new stage of life and about the origin of the tradition. In abbreviated form, I spoke about White Shell Girl and the intentions of the Holy People, emphasizing how everyone's presence would benefit Isaiah, as well as our family.

A line formed as Isaiah sat on his mother's lap and listened calmly to the various wishes of his guests. Lloyd helped him place salt in their palms and, after they had pronounced their wishes, offer gifts and fruit. As each person knelt in front of him, Shisóí was calm and quiet. Perhaps as White Shell Girl did, he was beginning to understand his role as a Diné person.

After this, Misty and Lloyd rose and thanked everyone for their expression of support and caring in their son's upbringing. Isaiah's aunt Lori also spoke about the meaning of such events in a child's life, and Bob and I expressed our gratitude. As people left, Isaiah stayed with his parents at the door to bid farewell to everyone. As if on cue, when the last guest departed, he began whimpering and wiggling to get out of his father's arms. We laughed as the children took him to join in their play.

We began to clear the kitchen and restore the house to its usual state; the ceremony was reassuring in many ways.

As mentioned earlier, this ceremony was first performed for White Shell Girl, who grew to become Changing Woman. It was said that White Shell Girl was the first Diné to have human form. Before she existed, our ancestors journeyed through three prior worlds and did not acquire physical form until they emerged in the present fourth world. (In some stories, this world is referred to as the fifth world, depending upon the storyteller and his or her age and on regional differences.) They were then called the Nihooką́ą́' Dine'é, or Earth Surface People, because the Diyin Dine'é, the Holy Ones, decided that this was where the Diné would live. The designation as Earth Surface People is linked with White Shell Girl because, in some accounts, when First Man found her, she did not assume human form until she was placed in First Woman's arms.

In a more familiar version, it is said that there were three worlds through which the original Diné and various beings journeyed before they emerged into the fourth world in northwest New Mexico. These worlds were black, blue, yellow, and white. The journeys were filled with fear, starvation, hunger, and other dangers. Unseen holy beings guided the people through each world as they experienced warfare, chaos, and other extreme perils. As they traveled, they realized that their survival, and that of their descendents, depended upon the knowledge and wisdom they acquired during this time. They attained skills such as tool making, food preparation, farming, and hunting; they also learned that respect for all living things was essential. This early body of hané comprised the origin of Diné philosophy and teachings and demonstrated that the ability to remember, to pay attention to details — including landscape and language — and to relay this information accurately was crucial.

The experiences of the people during this journey shaped aspects of contemporary life. For instance, the origin of the sacred mountains evolved when Áłtsé Hastiin, or First Man, took a handful of soil as he left each world. And when the group emerged in the fourth world, First Man had handfuls of black soil, blue soil, and yellow soil — the colors of the previous worlds — in his medicine pouch. When the Diyin Dine'é, the Holy People, began to conceive of a home for the people in the fourth world, they placed the soil in the center of the four mountains that they created to serve as boundaries of Dinétah. Blanca Peak was set in the east and is white (which represents the fourth world); Mount Taylor in the south is blue; the San Francisco Peaks in the west are yellow, and the La Plata Mountains in the north are represented by black soil. There are additional sacred mountains, but these compose the primary four.

The Diyin Dine'é exemplified the importance of thinking tasks through carefully and initiating responsibilities with the future in mind. The rituals and beliefs that are associated with each stage of a child's life, including the First Laugh ceremony, were implemented with the idea of Ntsínááhákees, thinking, at their core.

As White Shell Girl grew, she was fed ordinary food as well as specific types of pollen that allowed her to mature quickly; thus corn pollen is considered "the food of the gods." When her menses began, a puberty ceremony, the first Blessing Way, the Kinaałdá, was held. There was much rejoicing, because it represented the renewal and rejuvenation of the earth. She then assumed the name of Changing Woman.

At some time after the Kinaałdá, her coming-of-age ceremony, Changing Woman became pregnant with twins, whose father was the Sun. Her sons, Born for Water and Monster Slayer, were raised at Dził Ná'oodiłii, or Huerfano Mesa. When the twins were young men, they set out to find their father, who put them through a series of tests to prove their worthiness. During this period, Spider Woman, a holy being, guided them and protected them from their father and the various monsters that roamed about. It was said that these monsters were a result of the people's misconduct in the previous worlds. In the end, the Sun provided the twins with magical tools so that they could slay the evil beings, therefore ensuring a peaceful fourth world for the Diné.

Years later, Changing Woman became lonely for human companionship, so she created people from her body, and the first four clans came into existence. These were called the Nihookáá' Dine'é, or Earth Surface People, to distinguish them from the Diyin Dine'é, the Holy People. Thus all clans originated from these original four, and today when one introduces oneself by one's clan, it is an acknowledgment of a fundamental link to Changing Woman and to the Holy People.

Shortly after Changing Woman created the Nihookáá' Dine'é, the Diyin Dine'é decided the time had come for the Nihookáá' Dine'é to inherit the earth. They left various drawings, primarily at Dinétah, so that the medicine people would have a source of knowledge and could retain essential songs, prayers, symbols, and stories. Changing Woman now resides in the center of the earth. The changing of the seasons and the stages of our lives remind us that, indeed, she is our mother and that all comes to life as she breathes.

The Diyin Dine'é, the Holy People, traveled by means of a rainbow to take their places in the sacred mountains; thus the word for mountain, *dził*, is very much like *dziil*, which means "to be strong" or "to possess strength." Thus mountains serve as literal reminders that, like our ancestors, we can persevere in difficult situations. Since the mountains are images of eternity, attaining old age is a worthy goal. The Holy People set the intricate and complex pattern of Diné life when they decreed that we should live here, but they took care to ensure that these concepts could be integrated into modern life.

Today, when a rainbow appears after a cleansing rain, we know that the Holy People have returned. When they return, they marvel at the growth of new spring plants, they revel in the laughter of children splashing in the fresh rain puddles, and like us, they inhale deeply of the sweet, clean air. We understand that a rainbow sparkles with particles of dew, pollen, and the blessings of the Diyin Dine'é. We exist within the radiant curve of their care and wisdom.

I Remember, She Says

"Grandma, there's a big blanket of snow here," she says excitedly.
I smile, marveling at how near voices can seem over the phone.
It doesn't seem that long ago that phone lines were finally installed
in my parents' house outside of Shiprock.
The years collapse into decades almost unnoticeably now.

Chamisa talks eagerly about writing assignments and dance practice.
She dances fancy shawl; bells tinkle as she leaps and turns;
shiny fringes sway, and silver designs glitter. I can imagine her absorbed
in the songs and drumbeats; her face damp with sweat and concentration.
She spent the night at her best friend Hannah's house;
they watched TV really late and read a whole Nancy Drew book.
Her 12-year-old life bubbles on and on with activity and noise.
She is so far away and yet remains immersed in my life.
I smile and imagine her dark eyes and long, straight hair,
all these miles away in Kansas.
Between Chamisa and me are low rolling hills frozen in snow;
silent, glistening plains beneath the cold, still sky;
and rivers that flow in spite of the huge, noisy chunks of brown ice.

But here, the evening is turning pink, and two quails are sipping delicately
from the front pond. They lean so far forward,
for a moment it seems they will tip headfirst into the water.
I tell Chamisa, and she says, "But Grandma, if you try to help them,
they'll get scared and fly away."
I can imagine her concerned frown.

The sounds of the city are distant, and the warm winter air
lingers around the flat, sand-colored homes.
Inside, the scents of dinner, the tinkling of flatware and dishes
underlie the low hum of ordinary evenings.
Televisions pulsate in the background as little ones balk at their meals;
parents negotiate tomorrow's plans amidst homework reminders
and hovering overdue projects at work.
They are relieved to have made it to the day's end.
They know that night's dark rooms hold
unforeseeable dreams and tender, delicious sleep.

Each evening, the mountains surrounding us glow gold,
then pink, then purple that deepens into soft black.
The mountains know such evenings will be only memories decades from now.
Memories that will bring the sudden, light ache of waiting tears
and a gentle pang to the depths of one's chest.
The mountains remember the tenderness with which they were created.
They remember the way the Holy Ones sang with such beauty,
it compelled them to rise out of the flat desert.

Around here, everyone tries to catch the sunset.
It is always different — streaks of bright purple; long, pink, luxurious clouds.
Magenta, fuchsia, crimson, amethyst: this is where these words were created.
I tell Chamisa about the colors of the sky, and she says,
"I remember, Grandma, when we sat on the front porch to watch the sun set."

I remember, she says.

Old Salt Woman

'Áłk'idą́ą́ jiní, at the beginning of Navajo time, 'Áshįįh
'Asdzą́ą́n Sání journeyed to Huerfano Mesa near the shallow river.
They said First Baby was healthy, but her cooing was not a song
of joy or wonder. Since a baby does not know sorrow,
Old Salt Woman was called. They said that the colors
of laughter, of light effervescence traveled with her:

she who is the primordial mother of the Salt Clan. But her
true essence became apparent in her autumn years. When 'Áshįįh
'Asdzą́ą́n was young, she found that the wondrous colors
of betrothal can also contain hues of betrayal. Her pain was like a river
of luminous beads worn smooth by tears and intense sorrow.
Over time, she was able to transform the grief into exquisite songs

of beauty. You can still hear traces of her sadness in the songs
of doves on still desert mornings. But that day at Huerfano Mesa, her
cheerful arrival made it clear that all such sorrows
were in the past. Old Salt Woman held the baby, then put a bit of 'áshįįh
into her mouth. Then she said, "Wooshíí, wooshíí," and a radiant river
of baby laughter filled the hooghan. It was like the colors

of early morning, of clear skies, of salt — like the intense color
of midnight. Thus the laughter of relatives eating together became a song
for the First Laugh meal. It was there, just above the San Juan River,
that First Baby first kicked and laughed. Everyone watched her

eyes glitter with happiness. Her small, chubby hands pressed 'áshįįh
into each person's palm as they whispered wishes to her. In this way, sorrow

would turn from our kinfolk. 'Áshįįh 'Asdzą́ą́n Sání remembered such sorrow,
so she invoked the melodious names of mountains and the ageless colors
of stones. She invoked the taste of fresh corn. Then the baby offered 'áshįįh,
a box of Cracker Jacks, and some fruit. These became the ritual songs
that keep families together and loneliness away. Perhaps it was her
radiant smile or tender baby touch in our palm that told us crystal rivers

of salt flow unseen beneath our feet. The hot sun and thin, brown rivers
at Dinétah remember the day when Old Salt Woman arrived without sorrow.
They watched as the baby became White Shell Girl. She emulated the colors
of sharing, laughter, and the joy of stories. She was surrounded by her
family and relatives, encircled by love. Today her lilting songs
guide us to old age. Like Old Salt Woman, we cannot live without 'áshįįh.

Yes, it's true that a river of angry words can darken love's radiant colors.
And one can't say "I'm sorry" in Diné; but careful words and old songs
can recall the joy granted White Shell Girl, who first blessed us with 'áshįįh.

New Boots

This happened some time ago. For us it seems like last year, but for the younger ones, it's a story for the "long time ago" file.

Herbert was a patriarch of the family and had been sick for a few months. When death came, it was sadder than anyone could have imagined. Maybe it was that he was one of the last of his generation. With his death, there was now only a sister, Mary, and a brother, also named Herbert. In those days, people were known by their Navajo names, and their assigned English names were of little importance. No family member had ever called them "Herbert"—a name that was used only at the hospital, the Social Security office, and other official places. They had been raised in the early 1900s in the area around Tsé Dígǫǫn along with numerous siblings, most of whom had now passed on. Thus, both Herberts were uncles, fathers, grandfathers, or great-grandfathers to everyone in the huge gathering at the funeral. It would be difficult to go to Tsé Dígǫǫn and not visit this Herbert.

His funeral was held in both Navajo and English, and the church was filled. Comments and acknowledgments were a formality, since everyone was aware that Herbert was of the generation that spoke only Navajo, and he had never been to school or belonged to a church. They knew the "real talking" would take place later in the day.

The burial was on family land near the base of the mountain. The caravan of cars followed the hearse across the flat desert. After about thirty miles of paved highway, they turned onto a narrow dirt road. Billows of red dust streamed after the line of cars. After two miles, the hearse swayed a bit, then stopped. The driver and the funeral-home director got out and walked around to inspect the vehicle. The relatives were concerned at first; then they realized it was only a flat tire. All the young boys and men who saw this disembarked from their various vehicles to help out. There were nine guys ready to do something. The funeral director was embarrassed but determined to handle the whole thing as professionally as possible. He was wearing a suit and tie, so before doing anything, he slipped on a pair of overalls that he kept for just such emergencies and put on his work boots. No sense in getting his shiny, new Nacona boots all dusty. The dirt was like fine red powder, and small puffs rose with each step or movement anyone made. With the aid of three of the men, he changed the tire; the rest watched or looked out into the distance at the mountains or the clear sky and talked amongst themselves. Then within a few minutes, the procession continued to the family plot.

The graveside service was brief, which was a good thing because the afternoon sun was becoming fierce, and everyone knew it wouldn't be long before those annoying, almost invisible black gnats would appear in swarms. While a gospel group sang, the funeral director went over to the canopy where Herbert's wife and daughter sat in the still-somewhat-cool shade. He leaned over to the eldest daughter and told her in a whisper that her father's clothes and the mementos displayed at the funeral were in the back of the hearse. He had learned long ago that it was best to communicate directly with the mother or the eldest daughters of a family. "It's unlocked," he said. "When you're ready, just get them." She nodded. As the service concluded and they began to fill the grave, the family rose and walked slowly to their cars. Herbert's daughter retrieved the items from the back of the hearse, and they proceeded to the house where the meal would take place.

There, the adults had grateful, though composed, reunions with relatives they hadn't seen in years, new in-laws were introduced and silently scrutinized, and the elderly were seated and waited upon.

It was always something of a mystery the way the women instantly fell into an organized cooking and serving mode. Within minutes of everyone's arrival, they had served Herbert's immediate family, assigned servers to vacant spaces behind the huge pots of food, and poured coffee and punch into little foam cups that stood in straight lines of exactly eight rows each. There were no noisy conversations or commands, the women spoke quietly and carried on entire conversations without even looking at each other. It was clear that the sadness of the event caused them to concentrate even more fiercely on the tasks before them. It was also common knowledge that once a woman reached her mid-twenties, this inscrutable and collaborative wisdom was somehow bestowed upon her and at all gatherings, it enabled her to perform in synchronization with other women to make sure everyone was served and fed.

Meanwhile, the children sized up their new-found kin. They still thought it was weird to meet someone their own age whom they had never seen before, only to find that he or she was actually a brother or sister, or worse (for the relative), an aunt or a grandparent. And then they would notice that they kind of looked like each other and maybe even acted the same. At first they would be shy, staying near their families or "real" siblings, but eventually they began tentative conversations, then arranged themselves in little groups and sat in the shade of the huge trees or beside the house. They knew that this was a time when they could not even think of headphones or video games. These events took all day, and the kids made the best of it. Eventually, after everyone was served, one of their mothers came out of the house and gave them a meaningful glance, and they all got up and filed inside, seemingly unaware of their huge pants swishing and dragging as they walked. They came inside and began to clear tables and wash dishes.

Inside the house, the "talking" — speeches commemorating Herbert's life — was winding down. Various family members and other relatives stood near the center of the room and talked of their relationship with Herbert. They began talking in a normal voice; then their tone became more formal — rhythmic and poetic. They spoke of memories and of lessons learned, at times almost crying, yet never losing their composure. They gave advice to the large gathering of kinfolk, and at times it sounded like prayer. To an outsider it seemed as if they had rehearsed or memorized all this, but it was spontaneous — this natural tendency for poetic cadence and flawless repetition. Therein was the assurance that simple words can be beauty flowing from the mouths of ordinary people.

After the dishes were washed and the house was in order, people came to Herbert's family to say good-bye, to hug them, and to cry with them. Each child and teenager came to shake hands and though some remained silent, they understood how this loss had brought the huge family together.

Herbert's family had disposed of his belongings a few days before, but there were still a few items that they had decided to give to various relatives. They asked Herbert, his brother, to sit with them, and unexpectedly, they handed him a pair of almost-new boots. "We wanted to give you these," they said. "They were your older brother's boots."

Later, at his own home, he found that the boots fit nicely, which was lucky because this Herbert was considerably shorter than his brother. He was pleased with how they looked and felt; it had been so long since he had had anything new just for himself. He smiled to himself and took a walk down the road to test them out. He wore them the next few days, even though he knew they were too dressy for everyday stuff: the post office or the flea market.

On the Saturday after the funeral, Herbert's widow and daughters came to his brother's home. He and his family were happy to see them, and as they settled in at the table with coffee and spam-and-potato sandwiches, they talked of the last few months and of how things had changed. They told humorous stories about things Herbert and his brother had done as teenagers.

After an hour or so, the daughter said, "'Éii yá," of which Herbert and his wife took immediate notice, though this was not outwardly apparent. This expression signals the real reason for one's visit.

"'Adą̄ądą̄ą' yesterday afternoon, the white man from the funeral home came to our house. We didn't know why, because everything was paid for. We made sure of that. He sat with us awhile, and after some time, he asked if we knew what had happened to his boots. He had left them in the back of that long car.

"We just looked at each other, but we didn't say anything. My mother said she'll try to find out, and then he left. After he left, we just looked at each other and started laughing.

"So that's why we're here — because we gave you that white man's boots. We thought they were your brother's, even though he never owned such good shoes. But his relatives were always buying things for him when he got sick."

Everyone was laughing by this time, and even more so when it turned out that Herbert was wearing the boots. After they calmed down a bit, Herbert got up and took them off. He had even bought new socks; they were still white and cushiony. He wiped the boots off and handed them over. They took them — still laughing a little — and said their good-byes. "I guess we'll go see that white man," his sister-in-law said smiling.

"Those were sure good shoes," Herbert said as his brother's family drove out of the yard. "The best I ever had."

The Holy Twins

Ours was a play-filled childhood; irrigation ditches ran deep
during the summers. We played in the water and dirt, then inscribed
ABCs and numbers onto the smooth ground. Our cat Polly died
of rabies; then all the pets had to be shot, some in the rib cage
as they thrashed in panic. There was a pink bruise
on my forehead from pressing against the wall. We couldn't figure

out how such a thing could happen. The dogs were steadfast figures
around the farm. They chased strange cars and sometimes invoked deep
panic among visitors and passersby. They had cuts and bruises
from scuffles with roaming packs. No tags were inscribed
with their random Navajo names. Snazzy was skinny; his rib cage
obvious through thin fur. He looked as if he might die

from hunger, but he ate like nobody's business. Who knew he would die
of rabies with the rest? The main thing was to figure
out how they contracted it, my parents said. We cried until our rib cages
ached; our eyes stayed swollen. This first loss was too deep
to even talk about. Decades later, I can finally describe
how that summer led us into a grief that felt like a bruise

that would last forever. But our neighbor suffered worse bruises:
their huge dog, named Dog, was the first to die
and was the cause of all this. Their home and fields are inscribed
in our memories as "the rabies place." Over time, they must have figured

it was too much to live down. Childhood losses run deep,
even though we are grandparents now. The memory is an invisible cage

of anguished sobs, gunshots, yelping howls, canine rib cages
exploding. Sometimes we reminisce and notice that the bruises
of grief have turned pale like smoothed-over scars. That initial deep
hurt was the start, we found, of how love could die
right before us, even as we watched: stunned figures
pleading for mercy, urgent prayers saying, "Let God's scribe

mark this down. We've paid our dues. Our hearts are inscribed
with loss after loss." For some reason, after everything, our rib cages
held up and continued to cradle tender hearts. They must have figured
that all the prayers and careful teachings would prevent bruises
that would weaken us. Our love for those homely animals was deep

and would figure in the knowledge that such bruises
aren't endless, and that our rib cages are not mere bones. One can die
from grief, so now we can describe loss and love as the Holy Twins.

Festival of the Onion

Fall mornings in Umbria are veiled with dew.
Roosters awaken the dawn. I hadn't heard that wake-up call since childhood.
And there is coffee that makes one happy to be alive —
delicate, tiny cups filled with the dark essence that means Italia!
to drink this is to start the day murmuring *grazie! Grazie!*

From the balcony where we eat breakfast, we see olive groves
cling to gentle hills in the distance,
transparent clouds pause and rest on the rises.
I breathe the crisp air and thank the Holy Ones.

Later, arias drift from a home nearby.
The cobblestone lanes are narrow and shiny from centuries of use.
Tiny roads weave between the old houses and castles.

Walls are worn smooth from the handiwork of families over the ages.
The round corners and the slight indentations convey
the tenderness of home and long-ago grandparents.

One evening we attended an onion festival in Camerino.
It was like a miniature Shiprock Fair without the dust and mutton.
Parking was tight, but by some miracle, our host Gaetano squeezed
his little car into a space even smaller than the car.
I say *miracle* because the actual maneuver
was a blur of loud arguing between our driver and concerned passersby —
furious gestures mixed with spontaneous groans and sighs.

All this within five minutes, then calmness reigned again.
We had spent the afternoon at Assisi,
and it became clear that St. Francis had extended his compassion to Gaetano —
who was received as if he were the mayor everywhere we went.
At this point, I no longer panicked at the ordinary Italian conversation.

The first time the whole table erupted into loud chaos,
it seemed that a great wrong had been uncovered.
I was alarmed yet grateful for the Diné inclination
for sustained silent observation.
After everything reached a fever pitch, calm instantly descended.
It was then I realized that they were only figuring out the tip
for the group's meal.

At Camerino, we wound our way to the plaza
where large tents bustled with music, lights, sizzling meat,
and huge pans of onions cooked in every way imaginable — and unimaginable.
The onion was the star, and we mere celebrants.

That was the night we lost Scott Momaday.
We left Spello and planned to sit together at one table.
As Gaetano negotiated for a table for 13,
the rest wondered out loud where Dr. Momaday was.
We called Carmen and Emma's cell phones to no avail.
The drive from Spello was a matter of maneuvering in the moonlight
through dark fields and rolling hills of olives, grapes, and fig trees.

The narrow streets and parking lots were searched.
Finally, there they were — strolling toward us —
all smiles and casual greetings.

"Where were you?" several voices demanded. "We thought you were lost!"
For Gaetano Prampolini, to lose Scott Momaday would be the end
of everything.

Again, there was a loud eruption of questions, interrupted explanations,
demands, and defenses. Throughout all this, Scott listened,
leaning on his new walnut cane. He didn't look lost at all,
but then, can a man be lost if he is accompanied by three women?

With the lost party in place, we sat down to revel in the joys of the onion
as the night sky above Camerino filled with smoke, music, laughter, and wine.
We ate, gratefully reunited, savoring all varieties of roasted meats,
succulent potatoes, flavorful vegetables, and crusty breads.
We happily paid tribute with each bite and each story
to the tangy, even sweet, presence of the onion.

Far Away

(This poem is accompanied by a song.)

Rita was at the trading post waiting to have her check approved. She stood over to the side while people moved through the cashier's line. Then this guy came over after buying a bottle of Joy detergent. He said smiling, "It's really sad to be alone, I found out. That's why I'm buying this: to wash my dishes alone." Rita was so surprised, she just said, "Oh." After he went out, the cashier said, "Aye. Is that all you can say?" Rita and everyone in line laughed. When Rita came out of the trading post, that guy with the Joy was gone. Where trading post at?

The traffic is awful at Shiprock Fair. You have to park on Friday night to get a decent spot for the parade. Most families have a traditional spot, and every year relatives and friends look for them there. Sometimes we sell coffee and pop from the back of the pickup, but usually we drink all the coffee ourselves and forget to pay. The kids get so excited and try to dance with all the dance groups that come by. They catch candy from the various floats. Hours later when it's all over, they're sweaty, sticky with candy, and grouchy. So we pack up the chairs, blankets, bags of candy and free stuff, and ease into the long lines of traffic. No matter where we want to go, it's slow going. It's easier if the traffic officer is a relative; then you can say, "She'awéé', my baby, let me in." Then they'll stop cars and let you break into line. Once in traffic, a friend said, "Shiprock Fair is not the only one, you know. Tuba City Fair is better than this." We all just looked at her and thought, where Tuba City?

When we were children, my mother always sat beside Daddy as he drove. He would open the door for her and help her in. Daddy had a dog named Sandwich that he really liked. Sandwich followed him everywhere, and sometimes he sat on the passenger's side when he and Daddy went places alone. Then one day, Sandwich leapt in before Mom and sat beside Daddy. After that happened three times, Mom said, "I'm not going anywhere with you if that dog sits in the middle." Daddy just smiled, then he fixed Sandwich a special place in the back of the pickup. Later, Mom got in, looked around, and said, "Where's that old dog?" Where that old Sandwich?

For once they went dancing in Albuquerque. It was perfect — not too smoky; a live band playing; smooth, uncrowded dance floor; attentive waiters — best of all, Leona's husband was a good dancer. They danced to almost every song, except after fast swing numbers when they caught their breath and sipped cold drinks. One night, after he went to the men's room, the band started playing "Check Yes or No." "Oh shoot, my favorite song," Leona thought. Just then, an open hand appeared, requesting a dance. She glanced up and saw that it belonged to a tall cowboy. "Please," he said smiling. "No, thank you," Leona said. All of a sudden, he fell to one knee and said, "Just one dance, I'm begging you." Then he took his hat and pretended to clear a wide path to the dance floor. She just smiled. Then he leaned over and whispered, "Remember you broke my heart," and left. Why break his heart now?

I bought an old ts'aa' at the flea market.
My mother held it up to the afternoon sun to show its tight weave.
"You'll use it for a long time," she said.
We looked at jewelry, exquisite rugs, pottery, fine velvet cloth.
We lingered, musing over details.
Nearby was what we craved — snow cones.
The sticky sugar melted quickly.
Then we saw the Avon lady and got serious.

That American Flag

"I wouldn't buy anything with the flag on it," my friend said
as I showed her a cute straw handbag at Mervyn's one summer night.
It had a small beaded flag in the corner. *→ america is more than just the flag*
more history
"There's just something about me and the flag," she said. I didn't respond. *that is*
hidden by
Yes, the American flag is ubiquitous these days, *white*
and we had done our share of marches, protests, and sit-ins in the 1970s. *society*

But later that night, I wanted to call her and explain
about the American flag and us Navajos. *there is always another story/*
perspective
Let me tell you, I wanted to say, that in the mid-1800s
that flag meant fear and untold turmoil. *→ what the flag means*

Let me tell you, there was little we understood about those
who followed the American flag onto our land That thin rectangle of fabric
rippled in the dry gusts of wind as the troops approached Dinétah.
Though the men were five-fingered like us, their words *physical similarities*
seemed loud and careless, and their mannerisms, dramatic. *come*
Still, we watched for signs of compassion, *we all have families*
as these soldiers had been born of a mother somewhere. *from families*
Their mothers had been delighted to hear their first words,
just as some of these men must have talked to their firstborn soothingly.
Perhaps as they walked on Diné Bikéyah, they longed for their families.
These men walked upright, feet moving upon the earth's surface, as we do.
From childhood they had grown upward toward the sun as the Diné do.
They breathed the air granted all of us by the Holy Ones.
They were like us in these ways, but their hearts were unyielding.
They were faithful to orders from afar.

They were faithful to voices they had not heard themselves.
They were bound by written orders and armed with deadly gear.
They were loyal to their flag of freedom.

The government had decreed that the Diné be moved to <u>Fort Sumner</u>
so that we could become Americans. We traveled hundreds of miles
to the south. The winters were cold;
our blankets became worn and frayed.
Though we were given jackets, wraps, and clothing,
the sick worsened, the elderly passed on, and often babies died at birth.
At times the children played as children do anywhere;
other times they were listless from hunger and fear.
The men remained resilient: they talked late into the night
and sang quietly so as not to disturb the soldiers. They prayed
for the strength and insight to lead our people home.

The women set up looms, though they were immersed in grief.
"We have to weave as we always have," they said.
"By weaving, we can make it through these waves of sorrow."
"Someday we'll go home," they said.
"We have to weave through this hunger, through the pain,
through the deaths that surround us. We have to keep up
our strength," they said. "We have to weave
to remember our land, our relatives, and our animals."

→ redefine symbols of oppression

They unraveled the blue military jackets and red undergarments
and wound them into balls of crinkled wool.
They found bits of wool and cotton and sometimes sheep wool.
The military clothes became thin red and blue stripes in the rugs.

The stripes were laced, line by line — each weft tapped into place
by the weaving comb — its venerable echo a comfort in itself.
Sometimes they wove in strands of hair, feathers, bits of plants,
and knots of corn pollen to ensure strength and abundance.
These were offerings to the desolate land around them.
The rugs were prayers, with red, blue, black, and white stripes.

The rugs' white horizontal bands were for the early morning sky
and signaled new beginnings.
The background of the American flag is white,
as is our sacred mountain in the east.
Thus, the women knew we would survive.

The red stripes were for the dirt at home, the sandstone cliffs,
and for the sumac that turns brilliant red each fall.
The red stripes in the flag are for our blood and for our ancestors,
who tried to search for the good in everyone and everything.

By weaving blue into rugs, the women recalled the hooghans
they built when the men were gone. They recalled the graceful ease
with which their teenage sons chopped wood, built corrals,
and rode horses. In doing so, the women were reminded
of their own strength. The blue in the flag is for the promise
of each spring granted us since Fort Sumner. The blue stripes
honor the men and their strength, tenderness, and intellect.

Often, the women wove stars in the rug — its center is for our home,
Nihimá, the land that was given to us. We are told that
a specific star watches over us, this star knows everything.

The stars were prayers (for) the children, who held the future —
the ones who became our parents and grandparents.
The flag's stars signaled our eventual return to Diné Bikéyah.

When the clouds gather and darken over Dinétah,
the air becomes sweet with wet dirt, glistening sage, and creosote.
The black bands are like a woman's hair pulled back in a tsiiyéél,
which ensures clear thinking, guidance, and a wealth of songs and stories.

Sometimes the women wove crosses: a point
(for each direction and each of the sacred mountains.
The four points signal the hope that the changing light of each day brings.

Late that summer night, I wanted to tell my friend that
we Navajos have many reasons not to honor the American flag,
but often it reminds us of our grandparents' enduring courage.
In the face of terrible odds, the stars and stripes came to mean
that we would return to our homeland. It taught us that our mother,
Nahasdzáán, cares for us as we care for ourselves and our children.

redefine what the flag means to them

Let me tell you about the American flag and us Diné, my friend.
Let my grandparents: Shímásání dóó Shícheíí dóó Shináliké;
let them tell you about the American flag.

A Blessing

For the graduates of the University of Arizona

This morning we gather in gratitude for all aspects of sacredness:
the air, the warmth of fire, bodies of water, plants, the land,
and all animals and humankind.
We gather to honor our students who have achieved the extraordinary
accomplishment of earning doctoral or master's degrees.
We gather to honor their parents, grandparents, children,
family members, and friends who have traveled with them
on their path to success. They have traveled far distances to be here
this morning: we honor their devotion.

May we remember that holiness exists in the ordinary elements of our lives.

We are grateful for a homeland that has always thrived
on a glorious array of people and their diverse cultures, histories,
and beliefs. We acknowledge the generosity of the Tohono O'odham
in granting this land on which we learn, teach, celebrate
accomplishments, and sometimes mourn losses.

May we always cherish our ancestors as we prepare for the days ahead.
May we remember that we exist because of their prayers and their faith.

We are blessed with distinct and melodious tongues.
Our languages are treasures of stories, songs, ceremonies, and memories.
May each of us remember to share our stories with one another,
because it is only through stories that we live full lives.

45

May the words we speak go forth as bright beads
of comfort, joy, humor, and inspiration.
We have faith that the graduates will inspire others
to explore and follow their interests.

Today we reflect a rainbow of creation:
Some of us came from the east, where bright crystals of creativity reside.
They are the white streaks of early morning light when all is born again.
We understand that, in Tucson, the Rincon Mountains are our inspiration
for beginning each day. The Rincons are everlasting and always present.

Those who came from the south embody the strength of the blue
mountains that encircle us. The Santa Ritas instill in us
the vigorous spirit of youthful learning.

Others came from the west; they are imbued with the quiet, yellow glow of dusk.
They help us achieve our goals. Here in the middle of the valley, the ts'aa',
the basket of life, the Tucson Mountains teach us to value our families.

The ones from the north bring the deep, restorative powers of night's darkness;
their presence renews us. The Santa Catalina Mountains teach us that,
though the past may be fraught with sorrow, it was strengthened
by the prayers of our forebearers.
We witnessed the recent fires the mountains suffered,
and in their recovery we see ourselves on our own journeys.
We understand that we are surrounded by mountains, dziił,
and thus that we are made of strength, dziił, nihí níhídziił.
We are strong ourselves. We are surrounded by mountains
that help us negotiate our daily lives.

May we always recognize the multitude of gifts that surround us.
May our homes, schools, and communities be filled with the wisdom
and optimism that reflect a generous spirit.

We are grateful for all blessings, seen and unseen.

May we fulfill the lives envisioned for us at our birth. May we realize
that our actions affect all people and the earth. May we live in the way
of beauty and help others in need. May we always remember that
we were created as people who believe in one another. We are grateful,
Holy Ones, for the graduates, as they will strengthen our future.

All is beautiful again.
Hózhǫ́ nááhasdłíí'.
Hózhǫ́ nááhasdłíí'.
Hózhǫ́ nááhasdłíí'.
Hózhǫ́ nááhasdłíí'.

Late This Morning

Late this morning, a coyote howled somewhere nearby;
its prolonged tenor echoed in the light, silent rainfall.
I stopped writing and listened.
Birds began to chatter; then the neighbor's dog took up
the confused resonance of the morning.
"What is wrong," I said and stepped outside to listen.
But beyond the backyard, there was only wet dirt and plants glistening with rain.
The sweet scent of refreshed creosote filled the cool air.
Right there, the paloverde and cacti were soaked;
fat, clear beads of rain clung to their thin branches and narrow spines.
The teddy bear cholla were swollen; their white bristles brightened.
They seemed more stately as they strained skyward.

The howling stopped after a few minutes, and I continued
my usual routine: coffee, write, revise, read aloud, more coffee, edit.
The dim, still morning passed.

At noon I called my sister.
"Better get something done," she said urgently.
I know she is filing patient records in swift, repetitive motions.
I murmur in agreement.
Later, on the front porch I am immersed in the long, hushed pause of rainfall.
To the south, the city is beneath a dense mass of clouds,
and I remember the last time I heard coyotes —
their howling awakened us
in the early morning, and I stood then at the glass door

and peered out into the moonlit desert.
There seemed nothing unusual, yet the raw baying
lingered in the background of my dreams
and remained a silent specter throughout the day.
Now hummingbirds alight on almost invisible branches;
they keep watch on the thick sky overhead.
They flit to the bright feeder and hover in
shimmering motions of resilient beauty.
The huge rocks in the yard are shiny and slick,
beaming in the rare chance to display their original splendor.

On days such as this, one notices the faint breezes
that stir the drenched trees and bushes.
Like everything else, the vigilant cacti are swollen with gratitude.

The Canyon Was Serene

Tonight as the bright moon fills the bed, I am certain that I can't rise
and face the dawn. Dreams of Chinle and the mountains urge me to drive
back to the rez. My family knows why I left, but my husband's gentle horses
must wonder where he went. Since it happened, there has been no way to weave
this loneliness and the quiet nights into that calm state called beauty.
Hózhǫ́. Maybe it doesn't exist. These days it makes me sad and jealous

that some Navajos really live by hózhǫ́ǫ́jí . Yes, I am jealous
of how the old ways actually work for them. They wake, rise,
and pray each morning, knowing that they are blessed. For me, the Beauty
Way is abstract most of the time. At dawn, I rush out and drive
to work instead of praying outside. They say we should weave
these ancient ways into our daily lives. Do you remember the horses

his mother gave us at our wedding? Those horses
were such exquisite animals. We heard that people were jealous,
but we dismissed it. Back then, I rode horses for hours and used to weave
until sunset each day. Once we went camping in Canyon de Chelly. The moonrise
was so bright, we could see tiny birds in the brush. The four-wheel drive
got stuck in the sand, and two guys helped push it out. That night the beauty

of the old canyon, the moon, and the surprise rescue proved that the beauty
the elders speak of does exist. Late that night, a small herd of wild horses
came to our camp. They circled and sniffed the worn-out four-wheel drive.
It smelled of gas and sweat. The canyon was serene. It's easy to be jealous

of the people who live there. How much more substantial the sunrise
blessings seem there. During those summers, it was easy to weave

that story and many others like it into my rugs. Back then, I used to weave
and pray, weave and sing. The rhythm of the weaving comb meant that beauty
was taking form. Nights like that and his low laughter made my rugs rise
evenly in warm, delicate designs. Once, I wove the colors of his horses
into a saddle blanket. He teased me and said that his brother was jealous
because I had not made him one. Often memories of his riding songs drive

me to tears. Whatever happened to that saddle blanket? Once, on a drive
to Albuquerque, the long, red mesas and smooth cliffs showed me how to weave
them into a rug. I was so happy. Here, I was sometimes frustrated and jealous
of weavers who seemed to live and breathe designs. I learned that beauty
can't be forced. It comes on its own. It's like the silky sheen of horses
on cool summer mornings. It's like the small breezes, the sway and rise

of an Appaloosa's back. Back then, we drove the sheep home in the pure beauty
of Chinle Valley twilight. Will I ever weave like that again? Our fine horses
and tender love caused jealousy. He's gone. From his grave, my tears rise.

Long ago, the Holy People made the cradleboard,
saying, "By this rainbow, we shall return.
Lie upon your mother, the earth.
The cross board is your father, the sun."
They covered us in blankets of yellow, blue, white, and black clouds.
Sheet lightning and lightning bolts crossed over.
Now our parents carry us. Rainbows watch us.
Sacred clouds and lightning bolts hold us.

A Tune-Up

When Emma was a child, her family often took long walks on summer evenings after supper. The huge, old cottonwoods alongside the dirt roads were refreshingly cool after the long days of playing in the sun or working in the fields. They lived outside of town, and since electric lines had not yet reached their home, the moonlight lit the evenings. While the parents talked of ordinary things — childhood memories or visits to relatives — their footsteps crunched on the dirt road. The children searched for the Big and Little Dipper and asked again for the story in which the stars had once been people who had left this world for various reasons and now remained above, keeping watch. And though the distance between the earth and the stars was beyond measurement, it was said that the stars thought of the people as loved ones.

Often in the fall, when the entire family went piñon picking or camping, the children and women stayed at the campsite. During these trips, the girls slept with their mothers in the pickup bed. The boys and men slept in bedrolls around the fire. The children lay under warm blankets and whispered to each other in the chill mountain air. The tall pines swayed and rustled with the light breezes. The campfire smoke lingered in thin, white spirals and carried the voices and murmurings into the forest. Emma imagined that someone else far away would eventually hear the quiet voices of her family as the sounds drifted with the mountain breezes until early morning.

As a child, Emma considered the night to be intertwined with old stories and familiar voices. Occasionally, the children had overheard stories about ghosts and mysterious sightings of animals, but they were not included in these tellings. The adults' voices became low and hushed; a sure sign that the stories were not for children.

Emma's perception of such stories changed when she and her sisters enrolled at a boarding school during junior high school. They were among the two hundred Navajo girls who came from all over the reservation. The school housed all grades, and Emma's dormitory, like the others, was a low, angular, pale-green cement building. And her room was in a wing that extended from the center where the rumpus room and offices were. The boarding school introduced Emma to a new realm of storytelling — the kind her parents and relatives did not share in her presence. During those years at boarding school, after nightly bed checks and lights out, she heard stories that were both frightening and exciting.

Sometimes she wished she were not in the same room with the storytellers, who were her friends and as interested in becoming cheerleaders and attaining the honor roll as she was. In these stories, the night became dangerous and foreboding, and darkness presented opportunities for all kinds of strange and frightening events. Emma had always been afraid of the dark, even when she was with others; but during this time when she was in a room with seven other girls, anxiety became as familiar to her as the cool, taut sheets on her bed.

Late one night, several girls saw a figure near the top of the huge, steel water tower outside and said it had skimmed down quickly, unlike the manner of a human. The girls were whispering, gathered on a bed below a window. The dorm windows didn't have curtains or blinds and there was a clear view of the surrounding hills and mountains. Another time, three girls were leaving the dorm for breakfast duty when they saw four women standing atop the dining hall roof. The chow hall, as they called it, was below the dorm, which was on a slight rise. The morning was clear and cold, and the women on the roof stood close together as if in deep conversation. They wore Pendleton shawls, and only their heads were uncovered. When the girls saw this, they propped the heavy metal door open and called in loud whispers to their roommates, who ran to see the unusual sight. Then, as they turned to close the door slowly so it wouldn't slam, the women were gone. It was as if they had turned into mist; they couldn't have walked off the edge of the roof. Besides, they asked, where would they get ladders so early in the morning?

The boarding school years had been a thorough indoctrination into a kind of storytelling that Emma and her siblings would have avoided if given the chance. To counter this, their parents had given them subtle means of protection such as prayers, protection songs, corn pollen, and arrowheads: all methods of the Hózhǫ́ójí, or the Beauty Way, and a bit of Hózhǫ́ójí, protection against the bad. It was important that these things weren't obvious, as the school officials had strict rules against students possessing items that were distinctly "Indian." They appeared to have had no idea of the events or stories that were at the root of intense homesickness for many of the students. This deep longing for security often led students to run away from school.

Many years later, Emma enrolled at the University of New Mexico in Albuquerque and became close friends with Christine, a Navajo woman, who lived at Tó Hajiileehé, a small reservation town 30 miles west of Albuquerque. When she and Christine discovered they were clan sisters, their connection was immediate. One evening after classes, Emma and her two children visited Christine and her family and enjoyed a leisurely supper. They cleaned the kitchen, and it was almost midnight when they sat at the small kitchen table, eating piñons. Christine said that a strange being had appeared a few nights ago. That night her dogs began to bark, even as Christine peered out the windows, but she couldn't see anything or anyone. The dogs growled and bared their teeth at something they had trapped near the back window.

"I was so scared," she said, "just knowing that something or someone was so near, and that I couldn't see it."

The dogs growled and barked almost to a pitch of hysteria; then finally, after several minutes, the dogs chased the person or animal into the surrounding desert. They returned half an hour later, thirsty and panting loudly. As Christine shared this story, Emma reached into her purse for the pollen she kept. She held it, then said, "You shouldn't have told me that. Now I have to drive home alone with the kids." They both laughed nervously.

"It'll be okay," Christine reassured her, nodding toward the cellophane-wrapped corn pollen.

Such things happened often on the isolated reservation. Although one can see for miles, the small trees and shrubs can provide hiding places. The nights are pitch dark, especially when there is no moonlight, because there are few streetlights.

It's a well-known fact that homesite leases are a premium on the Navajo Nation. Yet, there are large expanses of available land for which no one applies—these are places where "all kinds of things happen" or areas that are "known for strange goings-on." These statements are vague, though the implication is quite clear: One should not ask questions or seek more information.

These accounts are the basis of the stories Emma had heard at boarding school; but later when she and her family moved to Albuquerque, stories of that type seemed irrelevant, as if they happened only on the reservation. Her fear dissipated in part because such things were rarely talked about among non-Indians. Emma spent the majority of her time with non-Indian classmates, as she was usually the only Indian in undergraduate and graduate classes. And later with colleagues, she realized that any kind of storytelling was rare among non-Indians; thus the telling of stories, for her, became relegated to her own family, visits to the reservation, or when she was with other Indian people.

Several years later, Emma took a teaching position in Nebraska: a position for which she, her husband, and their children moved reluctantly. But they understood that it was temporary and for her career. One evening, Emma stayed late at her university office — returning calls, grading papers, and catching up on tasks. She was so immersed in her work that, when she looked up, she was shocked to see that it was 6:15. The winter sun set early, and it was dark outside. In a mild panic, she picked up the phone to call home and was astounded to hear a Navajo voice. As she listened, a man was talking about driving to Window Rock, Arizona, which was hundreds of miles away. Someone else murmured "aoo'," a Navajo affirmative response. From Emma's office one couldn't get a dial tone without pushing "9" for an outside connection. Emma listened in disbelief and set the phone down quickly. She glanced around the office, then left, not bothering to straighten her desk, or turn off the computer or lights. She walked, shivering, down the long, quiet corridor of the humanities building. It felt as if she were watching herself, trying to hurry, yet not wanting to appear frightened.

The voices stayed with her for days. The man sounded so familiar, like one of her brothers or her friends or even her father. It was unnerving. She couldn't rationalize the fear. Besides her husband, no one else quite understood her fear. Her husband, who was not Navajo, had heard of other similar incidents occurring among his people and knew of its seriousness.

One of Emma's friends said, "It was probably an electrical problem; it happens all the time."

"But over 700 miles of telephone lines?" Emma had responded. She felt that she would have known if there were other Navajos in the small university town. She told no one else and went about her daily life as normally as possible. Finally, she called her brother one evening, and they talked for a long time. Her brother said that she should pray and try not to let it get to her, and that he would see what he could do. She felt better after hearing his voice and the low, slow-paced rhythm of Navajo.

Emma was familiar with the concept of being "pro-active," so she began praying — this time outside in the damp, icy dawn, not caring what her middle-class neighbors thought. She made náneeskaadi, tortillas, several times a week (previously it had been once or twice a month). Emma's mother had made náneeskaadi or fry bread daily, and maybe this was why, Emma became convinced, frightening events were rare in her childhood. Although she knew it wasn't rational, she thought that if she became more like her mother in her daily routines, she would be better able to ward off negative things. She sang and hummed Navajo songs. As it turned out, the more she sang, the more songs she remembered. She swept the kitchen and front porch each morning. She called silently upon the various Holy People for help before she began any task. Each night, she prayed until sleep came. It surprised her how little effort and time it took to add these things to what she had considered an overwhelming daily schedule.

One winter night, the neighbor's hounds began barking in the backyard. This barking sounded unusually intense compared to the usual barking that annoyed everyone on their street. Emma's husband glanced out the bedroom window.

"I wonder what they are barking at?" she asked.

"I don't see anything," he replied.

She joined him at the window, and in silence, they scanned the sprawling backyard. Then she remembered Christine's story. From the upstairs window, their view was partially blocked by huge, bare oak trees. Everything — the grass, shrubs, trees, and fences — was coated with thin, silver sheets of ice. It was hard to believe that anyone or any animal could be out on such a night. The freezing night was reassuring, though, because footsteps would easily be heard if anyone walked on the icy ground near the house. She fell asleep long after the neighbor's dogs stopped barking and was exhausted the next day.

The following evening, her brother called to say that he and her siblings had made arrangements for an all-night ceremony outside of Fruitland, New Mexico. Meanwhile, he cautioned her not to drive after dark. She agreed and didn't question his request. The next day was spent gathering some of the required items: canned corn and fruit, flour, potatoes, canned meat, and various other nonperishable foods, as well as two-yard lengths of velvet and calico fabric, and packaged blankets. Family members would also bring their share of the payment for the medicine man, as everyone would benefit from the prayers.

Emma cancelled her Friday class, citing a "family emergency." She was aware that, in fact, she was the "emergency," and she reminded herself not to act the part. She recalled her parents' composed behavior at critical times, and the memories calmed her. That evening they packed the minivan, and early the next morning, after praying, they began the long drive to New Mexico. As usual, the Midwest was fiercely cold, and had they not been going for a ceremony, the thick, gray skies and slick, black highways would have turned them back immediately.

They stopped only for gas and once in southern Colorado to replace a frozen fuel pump. Luckily, the pump gave out during daylight hours when they were near the city of Pueblo. The wind, combined with blowing snow, accompanied them to the New Mexico state line, and then the skies cleared, but it was still icy cold. The highways shone with black ice. Emma and her husband alternated driving, while the children slept off and on. When they woke, it was clear that they, too, were worried about this trip. But no one voiced their concerns aloud. To do so may have been to court bad luck.

In the afternoon of the second day, they arrived at Emma's parents' home, where the warm smell of piñon and cedar and the scents of various foods lingered throughout. They were all relieved to be back home; the children immediately huddled with their numerous cousins to play and catch up on the latest news. After they ate, the children had to nap, because the ceremony was a "no-sleep" and they would have to stay awake all night. They didn't protest as they might have otherwise, and soon almost everyone was asleep. Other siblings had driven in from Phoenix and Flagstaff, so they too were travel-weary — their tiredness compounded by the drive over cold, frozen roads.

Around seven that evening, after a noisy supper, everyone set out in several vehicles to the medicine man's home. Upon arrival, the family assembled along the walls of the round house and sat on the dirt floor or on blankets that were placed along the walls. Emma and her family sat on the west side as the "primary patients," and her parents sat on each side of them.

The warm hooghan was soon filled with long, rambling, rhythmic prayers and ancient monotonic songs. The medicine man prayed for Emma and her family, and they in turn prayed for themselves, as well as for everyone else. The prayers began in the center of the hooghan, where the medicine man sat behind the fire, and moved out to include Emma, her family, her parents, and all of the family who sat there in the dim darkness. Their faces were visible in the firelight. The fire crackled and sizzled. The prayers extended to include the six sacred mountains that surrounded the hooghan, and continued on to include the frozen winter air, the dark, ice-encrusted plants, the animals that were quieted by the cold, the tiny silent birds perched in the bare trees outside, the insects underground that were numbed by winter, the river nearby that tumbled chunks of ice, and the huge gray sky that covered and watched over everything. The rhythmic invocations included the Earth Surface People, the first ones to walk upon this land, and the grandparents of the elders in the hooghan — the medicine man called upon all their maternal and paternal grandparents from the beginning of time.

"Look upon your grandchildren," he said. "Nihinálíké dóó nihisóóké. They remember what you taught them. Thank you," he said to them, "for teaching us."

Throughout the night, Nahasdzáán was invoked; she who warmed them as they sat on that winter floor; she who had given them blessing songs — the songs of the female. Nahasdzáán, Mother Earth, the partner to the male protection songs. All night the songs and prayers lingered, then rose through the chimney into the cold air outside.

They were surprised when morning arrived; even the children were still awake. Only the littlest ones had fallen asleep. Though everyone was a bit tousled and their clothes were rumpled, they felt refreshed. Their minds were clear and serene. They smiled easily and were happy to go out with the medicine man for the last prayer. Emma could see their prayers rising in the cold, bright dawn. The prayers rose in symmetrical forms of shimmering hope.

"This is what it means to be restored," she whispered to her husband.

The remainder of the visit was filled with endless food, visits with relatives, stories, laughter, the children's shouting, crying, and weak protests against baths and washing before meals. At times, Emma and her siblings recalled their childhoods and teased each other about various escapades. No matter how many times the stories were told, the children loved to hear them again and again. They couldn't imagine their parents as children. Her parents presided over the series of events. They watched and listened as their children and grandchildren, and even two great-grandchildren, gathered to share laughter, fears, memories, and failures. They were reassured that no matter what might lie ahead, they seemed capable of handling it.

Emma and her family left early the next morning; it was still dark and the dirt roads were frozen. They prayed with her parents, and after hugs, and kisses for the children, they piled into the van. The children were quiet and sullen, but within half an hour, they were asleep.

They drove straight through again — back to Nebraska — right into the stinging, icy wind. At times they could barely see the highway. But they weren't as nervous; things were different now. There was a certainty with which they traveled; a tranquility in their conversations and in their actions.

"Finally, we can live the life we were given," Emma said to her husband.

He simply nodded as men do when there is no need to respond. He looked over at her, then squeezed her hand.

When they stopped for hamburgers in Denver, her son said, "Mom, having that Hózhǫǫjí, is like a tune-up. Huh? A tune-up for us — like the way Apple got a new fuel pump."

Emma and her husband laughed and agreed. Apple was the name of their van.

Then the children slept in the warm Apple as she moved smoothly through the frosty spaces of southern Nebraska. Under the snow the ground was solid, and above them the sky encircled them with icy crystalline air.

Red Star Quilt

Last night we slept with the windows open. The desert's breath
swept through the waiting spaces
of the dark house. The air smelled faintly of rainwater —
that refreshing scent that is mostly foreign
to the Sonoran desert. The clouds were billowing patches
above the Santa Rita Mountains. Such nights call for cold drinks

and stories on the front porch. Often young people drink
beside the Rillito to celebrate the fragrant breath
of the monsoons. Here in Pima County, it rains in patches
according to zip code. But in 2005, the rain outpaced
the record highs, and the Rillito and Santa Cruz Rivers looked foreign
as they roiled with brown, rushing waters.

Branches, toys, and plastic bags bobbed in the muddy water.
Inevitably each summer, someone who has been drinking
faces, then becomes outraged by, orange flood barricades — such foreign
dictators! Thus emboldened, they swear, breathe
deeply, and steer SUVs through the river. Surely they can outpace
the rushing Rillito. Minutes later, they are wet, pitiful patches

of humanity waving for help. The EMTs, who wear patches
of compassion woven on their shirts, maneuver into the water
on ropes and ladders. Early on, the EMTs learned to pace
patience with empathy. They've seen all that drinking

can do. To them, the long-awaited monsoons mean fewer breaths
of relaxation. The monsoons are beautiful, yet foreign.

Later, on fall nights when cool air and animal noises reign,
this same desert is a place where all the weary patches
of life come together. It's a long, drawn-out breath
after too many 100° days and cold water
faucets that run warm until November. A strong drink
can't soften the sudden break in the pace

of cooing bird calls: that pause when coyotes have outpaced
an ill-fated rabbit. The eruption of screams and cries aren't foreign
in the desert. In seconds it's all over, as whimpers reign.
That's life: adrenalin, grief, and loss all patched
together with memories and blood. Even so, coyotes sense rainwater
in the damp air as we, too, step outside and take deep breaths.

The clean breath of fall has finally moved into the daily pace,
and the scent of water and the sound of thunder are no longer foreign.
I cover the bed with a red star quilt. There is no need for drinks.

Journey of Turquoise

You are noticed immediately: smooth, bright ovals of turquoise
that attract a stranger's eye.
The teller at the drive-up window says, "What a beautiful ring."

He found you in the shade at a powwow market
in Idaho: round cluster ring made by a Tuba City Navajo.

He recognized you as one I would love, so he brought you to Kansas.
You're a traveler — Tuba City, Idaho, Kansas, Pecos, and now Tucson.
You're a traveling song: hours through stark, vivid deserts;
winding mountain roads; safe flights through calm skies;
detail-filled homecoming drive to our bright, restful house.

Your clear stones radiate this journey we make together.

Náneeskaadí

When the weather is nice, we sit under the trees with covered bowls
of warm dough and make bread on grills set over glowing ashes.
More often, we sit in my mother's kitchen
and take turns placing flattened circles of dough on the hot griddle.
The stack of bread alternately grows, then shrinks,
depending on how many people are around.

These days I drive home in the darkened evening to a quiet house.
The cats greet me with a glance and a yawn. They look repeatedly
at their food bowls; they want canned food. "It seems like everyone
wants something from me," I complain while filling their bowls.
Dexter Dudley Begay purrs in response. I wish for beans or warm stew,
but then I just wash my hands and line up ingredients,
as I learned to do in home economics years ago.
"Never start cooking without everything being in order,"
Mrs. Bowman preached.
I mix the dough and cover it, then let it set while
I change clothes, turn on lights, and fix a glass of ice water.
Then I search the refrigerator for something to accompany the náneeskaadí.
"It goes with everything and anything," my inner Martha Stewart reassures me.

The process is simple. Take a few handfuls of flour,
preferably Blue Bird or Navajo Pride.
Toss with a bit of salt and a palmful of baking powder. Mix well.
Ponder the next ingredient awhile, but then go ahead
and add two fingertips of lard —

not too much, just enough to help the texture.
Mix very well. Then pour in 1½ cups of very hot water
(as hot as you can stand) and mix quickly.
Mix until the dough forms a soft ball and the remaining flour
lifts away from the sides of the bowl. Rub olive oil on a griddle
and heat it until very warm; then take a ball of dough
and pat it into a disk. Stretch it gently,
while slapping it back and forth from hand to hand.

After a few minutes, a rhythm emerges from the soft, muffled slapping
combined with the pauses to lay the dough on the griddle, flip it over,
its removal from the hot grill, and its quick replacement.
Soon the kitchen warms, and the fresh scent of náneeskaadí drifts through
the house. The cats are now sleeping circles of fur; the door opens;
my husband comes in smiling. He is savoring náneeskaadí and melting butter.

"Na'. Here." As in "Na' k'ad yiłwoł. Here, now go run along."
"Ná. For you."
"Díí na'iishłaa. I made this for you."
"Na', díí ná iishłaa. Here, I made this for you."
"Ná 'ahéésh kad. I slapped this dough into shape for you."
"Díí náníinsííł kaad. This warm circle of dough is spread out for you."
"K'ad la'. There. Łikanish? Is it good?"

Near-to-the-Water

Most afternoons at Nííst'ah, when the sky is a brilliant teal,
Hánáábaa' is at the sunlit stove tending the speckled enamel pot.
The hooghan is redolent of simmering soup and blue corn meal.

As a child, Hánáábaa' learned to blend the fine corn meal in the still
mountain mornings. The quiet cadence of the stirring spoon brought
forth her mother's voice on those days when the sky was a brilliant teal.

Later when Tó'áhání saw the red sun set in Hánáábaa''s hair, it instilled
such an ancient longing — like the lilting grinding songs that wrought
childhood repasts: warm bread, simmering soup, and blue corn meal.

On quiet, cold nights, the elders tell of how a woman's long hair reveals
enduring wisdom. They say Changing Woman's hair averted drought
on a dusty, hot afternoon centuries ago when the sky was a brilliant teal.

For Tó'áhání, the glistening of Hánáábaa''s hair recalled the low peal
of distant thunder, when thin cornstalks rippled in dry fields and sought
cool rain. Now her hooghan is redolent of simmering soup and blue corn meal.

As Hánáábaa' stirs the enamel pot in the low winter dusk, her songs yield
memories of Tó'áhání: his resonant voice and dark eyes. The decades have taught
Hánáábaa' that those long-ago afternoons and the skies of brilliant teal
are the quintessence of stories, simmering soup, and blue corn meal.

Dawn Boy

It's almost 6 a.m., and the birds have began their clear
ritual melodies. They are the enduring voices
of children like Dawn Boy, the cripple, who smeared his skin
with colored clay. The children were abandoned one evening as daylight
faded; the little disfigured ones were forsaken in a brush arbor. Crow
existed then, and he watched quietly. The small arbor was faded by the sun.

In southern Colorado the mornings are glorious, but the noonday sun
can be harsh. Not unlike the children's parents, who were clearly
angered by their offspring's infirmities, though they too had flaws, crow's-
feet, and limps. That night, the arbor was cold, and their whimpering voices
and cries went unheard. They were considered burdens: deformed limbs, slightly
scarred skin, and two who were blind. Dawn Boy's leg dragged, and the skin

of his fingers merged into stubs. Though the children's baby skin
was flawless, it was blue with chills. One father had left his son
a blanket, which they huddled in. The dark sky arched above. Starlight
glistened. Though Dawn Boy was weak, it became clear
that at four he was the eldest, so he moved about the arbor, his voice
soothing as he wiped tears and runny noses. They ate bread bits. Crow

watched all this. Then as Dawn Boy hummed, Crow
suddenly interrupted — *gáagii, gáagii!* Dawn Boy sang, though his skin
grew chilled. He quieted fears, because the parents' angry voices
ushered in tearful nightmares. Finally, the hearty morning sun

rose, its rays glistening with dew; it signaled a warm, clear
day. The children woke hungry and disoriented. In the new light,

Dawn Boy led the disheveled little band toward the east. The lightest
one climbed on his back. They stopped at a lake and played. Crow
followed them. They made toys of clay and stood them to dry in the clear
sunlight. Then the Diyin Dine'é appeared to the children; their skin
was now mottled with white clay. For the next three days, the children left at sun-
rise and traveled south one day, then west, and finally north. Their voices

preceded them — subdued chatter or singing. Now their voices
were like those of cherished children. They moved easily, lightly.
On the fourth day, the parents crept behind, bewildered. At sun-
rise, they came to the lake where pale shells and toys glistened. Crow
waited. A rainbow appeared. The parents cried, gasping. Our kin-
folk were distraught as they watched the children run to the clear,

radiant embrace of the Diyin Dine'é, who turned them into tiny birds. Gáagii's
voice remained. Today their light eagle plumes tell us that marred skins
of hóchx̨ǫ́ǫ́ can fall aside. The children sing each sunrise; their absolution clear.

Tomorrow I will drive to Shiprock:

A day-long drive through saguaro-studded landscape,
dizzy with wildflowers, through frenzied Phoenix freeways,
beside ageless sandstone cliffs; and I will drive beneath
the San Francisco Peaks: our mother who was created by
the sheer beauty of holy singing at the beginning of Navajo time.

By nightfall, I arrive at my mother's home.
No matter how late, she waits for me.
I have to knock loudly because she doesn't hear well.
Her world is slightly muted with the low hum of vibrant memories,
the deep-rooted routine of ordinary tasks,
and our voices hover on the periphery of her daily life.

I walk through the doorway into her soft hug and quiet smile.
"Shimá, Shi isht'e," I say. My mother, it's me.
Sometimes she can't tell my sisters and me apart.
"Oh, She'awéé'," she murmurs.
My eldest sister has made fresh bread, and still-hot stew is on the stove.
We sit down, and they tell me about various relatives:
who was at the post office or at the city market; our uncle was sick last month;
the neighborhood kids were drinking and speeding again.
Later, two other sisters drive into the yard, and after knocking,
they enter in a flurry of smiles, loaded with armfuls of warm food,
cold pop, and plenty of teasing laughter.

After I have asked a few times about her health,
my mother says, "I'm doing okay, She'awéé'.
There's enough wood and coal. The ones-with-whom-you-were-raised
and my grandchildren keep an eye on me.
They really take care of me," she says. "T'áá ako ndi yée'."

"I'm getting used to being alone," she says, and we all pause.
My throat aches at the mere mention of nihzhé'é — your father.
Shizhé'é. Shizhé'é yée. My father.

What a deep, clear voice he had.
"I used to like to listen to him," I say, touching my mother's arm.
She looks at the vinyl tablecloth and says nothing.
Her eyes glisten, but she does not cry.
We sit like that and remember his voice
as he reminisced about decades long gone, as he made plans,
told jokes, or as he made house repairs or worked in the fields.

He is here; he is here with us.
We are surrounded by his silent comfort.

We eat, then clear the dishes. "Don't wash them," my sister says.
"They can wait until morning."
"Ch'ééh dínyá shíí" my mother says.
"You're probably tired. Get some sleep."
We settle into the bedtime routine: brush our teeth,
talk about tomorrow, scold the cat, and finally we retire.

My mother's home is the same:
a dark, quiet haven of long-ago dreams,

a reminder of adolescent disappointments,
a refuge from failed relationships,
and the long, deep realization of full lives lived.

As I fall asleep in the house of my childhood,
I hear my mother turn over in her sleep; and as her breathing evens out,
my past and future merge in the dark, still air.

Tsílii

Sometimes this guy just makes me laugh.
Just as easily, he can make me see red,
like when he tries to take off as if he thirsts
for freedom. Actually, he needs me like a dog
needs a pack. Besides, he loves my crew-cab truck.
When he first noticed my jewelry, I became the woman

for him. Not only that, but because I'm a Diné woman,
his life revolves around me. Now he recognizes my laugh
from a distance. Some evenings we go for rides in the truck
down winding River Road as the sky fills with purple and red
streaks. To the south, people walk along the Rillito, their dogs'
noses bent to the ground. The dogs are excited and thirsty.

A Diet Coke is enough to quench my thirst.
In the Southwest, the quintessential pleasures for women
are a faithful car, good music, and good stories. We're not dogged
by having to drive hundreds of miles; we just reminisce, laugh,
and sometimes sing. During trips north to
Shiprock, dusk turns everything red,
as the vast Salt River Canyon welcomes my truck.

It is as we used to say, we "keep on trucking"
through whatever may come our way. Our thirst
for stories and laughter never ceases. Once I read
that animals make life complete; but a woman

like me needs more than that, I thought and laughed.
Then I remembered the cats, rabbits, chickens, and dogs

of my childhood. How Lobo, Snazzy, and Tłog'í didn't seem like dogs.
They listened, ever alert, while lying under Daddy's truck.
They probably never really slept. Sometimes they even seemed to laugh
when we spoke English. But back to this other guy, he thirsts
to be near me — even when I'm driving. "Move over," I say. "A woman
needs space and no distractions. Sit on your side before red

lights come flashing! I'll be handcuffed and read
my rights, and you won't even care! Act like a dog
and look out the window!" I scold. He knows when a woman
means business. He moves slowly over to the passenger-side
door and looks at me — his dark, shiny eyes thirsty
for affection. He gets the same look when I laugh

unexpectedly; and he doesn't laugh when I talk English like those rez
dogs. But those dogs instilled in me a thirst for a sleek little dog,
a tsílii, who likes trucks and lives only to make his mom a happy woman.

Elegy for My Younger Sister

For Marilynn

Nihideezhí, it was a moist June afternoon when we buried you.
The Oak Springs Valley was dense with sage, cedar, and chamisa;
and gray, green, and brown shrubs cradled the small cemetery.
The sky was huge overhead.
Your son said later, "Did you see the sky? It was purple.
I knew it would rain," he said.

The dark Carrizo Mountains were so clear.

There were so many people, Sister.
Many of your friends whom we didn't know,
and your former schoolmates whom we remembered as children,
and Sister, we met many relatives for the first time.

We cried, not wanting to leave you in that serene place.
We hesitated, though our father, his parents, and their parents
are buried there. Our older sisters thought ahead to bring flowers for them.
They huddled quietly over their graves a few feet away.

Shideezhí, remember how red the sand is?
The men — your sons, our nephews, grandsons, and various in-laws —
took turns filling your grave. Their necks and arms were streaked
with dusty sweat. They kept their heads down;
their faces were damp and eyes, swollen.

We had to get it all out; we cried
and held each other. My granddaughters hovered near me
as if I might faint or fall unexpectedly.

Did you see, Sister, the way the grandchildren fed and served everyone?
They guided the grandparents and the elderly to their chairs.
Once seated, they served plates filled with mutton ribs,
potato salad, corn, thick slabs of oven bread, crispy fry bread,
and Jell-O salad. They placed the salt and pepper — that enduring couple —
before us and implored us to eat. The two delights we relished were good —
hot, strong coffee and cold, crisp diet pop.

We ate for you; we consumed your meal, Shideezhí.
We ate to honor the times you cooked for us —
those tasty dishes, scrumptious pastries combined with laughter,
silly childhood memories, and always teasing jokes.
Sister, I didn't know how we would make it;
it is still too much to think of you not being here.

K-Tag Ceremony

In the summer of 1999, we hugged our children and their children
and headed west out of Lawrence, our cars packed full.
Our K-Tags waved us onto the turnpike for the final time.
Bob and I drove separate cars and followed each other through the lush hills.
The cats howled until the sedatives took over. We had left the house
that cared for us for ten years. It was clean and empty.
It was a good Diné hooghan that greeted the Holy Ones each morning.
They arrived cloaked in rain, slants of heavy snow, thick veils of sunlight,
shiny sheets of ice, or sometimes drenched in heavy summer heat.

The Holy Ones named our grandbabies as we presented them
to the sun, our father, their little arms extended to the south and north.
They shivered in white baby shirts. Over the years,
the front porch became layered in prayers and first baby steps.
Sometimes as I watched the little ones collect acorns or tug at lilacs,
I yearned for my mother to sit beside me.
I longed to hear my father sing one more time.
Then one June night, we returned here after we buried him, Shi zhé'é.

It was the same porch that welcomed friends who arrived laden
with food and bottles of drink, and full of stories, gossip, and laughter.
How many hours of *Twin Peaks* did we ponder in the den?
How many times did the den almost burst with Jayhawk enthusiasm?
How many times did Helen fall asleep on that couch?

Often, chance blessings drifted to our house in the echo
of powwow drums and singing. Through the window screens,
the ageless rhythm that sustains our relatives, the Plains people,
lulled us to sleep. The old singing gathered us in, ensuring another sunrise,
while outside, tiny fireflies flickered under the huge oak trees.
Nearby, the dark creek brimmed with tiny fish, otters, and raccoons.

The morning we left Lawrence, the moist summer air glistened good-bye.
We surrendered the K-Tags in Wichita. It seemed to call for a ceremony
of some sort, but we were simply thanked and the passes, tucked away.

Perhaps it was clear that we would return; maybe our faces mirrored
the intensity of our years in Kansas; maybe the celebrations and losses
were evident in our eyes. After all, our children were grown,
and we were returning to my mother and to my home country. I was close
to tears, but then Bob smiled at me — his eyes were clear and calm.

So I adjusted the car visor, slipped in a fresh audio book,
and began a whole new story.

The round-roof hooghan is like a woman's tiered skirt.
It is said that the mother, amá, is the heart of the home.
    It is said that there is beauty within,
      when a home is as it should be.

matriarchal society

    Beauty extends from the hooghan.
    Beauty extends from the woman.
    Beauty extends from the woman.
    Beauty extends from the woman.
    Beauty extends from the woman.

The Way to Tsé Bit'a'í

The family lived at Tsé Ntsaa Deez'áhí. The men had gone hunting north of Lók'a'jígai and took note of the good grazing and farmlands. So they bartered with the trader for two tsíínaabąąś, horse-drawn wagons. The relatives asked them to leave a wagon for their use, but my grandmother refused. She thought of her teenage sons and little daughters. "We can't," she said. "We don't know what lies ahead." They left with 63 head of sheep and some horses. Everyone gathered as they moved away slowly in the clear morning air. Some cried and others simply watched. Then they laughed, because the baby's head was barely visible above the brush. Her head was a little black dot moving behind the sheep. Two days later, the family had crossed over the Carrizo mountain ridge and settled at Nííst'ah. To the east, Tsé Bit'a'í was a sentinel above the flat land.

After the forced removal of the Diné in 1864 to Fort Sumner, the treaty signed upon their return in 1868 stipulated, among other items, that livestock be distributed among the survivors of the Long Walk. Akinabah Burbank said, "Then, the White Men told the people, 'Now you are on your own, go your way; now that you have some sheep, take care of them.'" The federal government chose to add to the Diné land base and to contribute to the numbers of livestock owned by the people. "The Diné did not for a moment ever doubt the appropriateness of their movements. They had come home or come out of hiding and begun the process of reclaiming a homeland. They would never forget the events of this time of troubles, but at the same time, they could now begin to look to tomorrow. They went about the demanding but ultimately fulfilling process of expanding their holdings of livestock and claiming the land and water resources necessary for their animals. In a larger sense, as the people built new hogans, began new families, and acquired new livestock, they started to believe in a future that only recently had seemed impossible to realize."

This morning before dawn, the dissipating night sky is silver. The ridges of the Santa Catalina and Santa Rita Mountains are distinct. They encircle our home and the surrounding yards of cacti and bright paloverde. The fine hair on my arms stands upright with the morning chill. Hundreds of miles to the north, my mother has awakened. She rises slowly and sits for a few moments at the edge of the bed. She walks in the quiet to the front-room window and offers a silent prayer. Frost glistens on the trees. Then she turns and warms herself by the first fire of the day. Early each morning I know she thinks of me, just as I imagine her and recall the slow and careful way she moves about the kitchen. I can see the filtered sunlight streaming through the frosted window.

We
must remember the worlds
our ancestors
traveled.
Always wear the songs they gave us.
Remember we are made of prayers.
Now we leave wrapped in old blankets of love and wisdom.

acknowledgments

The following poems have appeared in the publications listed:

"I Remember, She Says." In *Lasting: Poems on Aging*, ed. Meg Files, 112.
Tucson, Ariz.: Pima Press, 2006.

"The Radiant Curve: Navajo Ceremony in Contemporary Life." In *Native
Universe: Voices of Indian America*, eds. Gerald McMaster and Clifford E.
Trafzer, 263–73. Washington, D.C.: National Museum of the American
Indian, Smithsonian Institution, in association with National Geographic,
2004.

"The Canyon Was Serene." In *Poems*. Glencoe Literature Library: Native
American Literature. Woodland Hills, Calif.: Glencoe/McGraw-Hill, 2002.

"The Warp Is Even: Taut Vertical Loops Between Our Father and the Earth"
and "Old Salt Woman." In *In Company: An Anthology of New Mexico Poets
After 1960*, eds. Lee Barlett, V. B. Price, and Dianne Edenfield Edwards,
252–59. Albuquerque: University of New Mexico Press, 2003.

"Earthwords: Nine Poems and Essays." In *Here, Now, and Always: Voices of the First Peoples of the Southwest*, ed. Joan K. O'Donnell, 22. Santa Fe: Museum of New Mexico Press, 2002.

"Near to the Water." In *Red Ink* (Tucson: University of Arizona American Indian Studies Program) 8, no. 2 (2000): 53.

Akinabah Burbank's quote in the second paragraph of "The Way to Tsé Bit'a'í" is from *Diné: A History of the Navajos*, text by Peter Iverson, photographs by Monty Roessel, 67. Albuquerque: University of New Mexico Press, 2002. The second quote in this paragraph is also from *Diné* (p. 69).

about the author

Luci Tapahonso is originally from Shiprock, New Mexico, and is a professor of American Indian Studies and English at the University of Arizona in Tucson. She is the author of three children's books and five books of poetry, including *Blue Horses Rush In*, which was awarded the Mountain and Plains Booksellers Association's 1998 Award for Poetry.

Professor Tapahonso is the recipient of a number of other awards as well, including the 2006 Lifetime Achievement Award from the Native Writers Circle of the Americas. She and her husband, Robert G. Martin, live in Tucson and Santa Fe.

contents of audio cd

This book includes an audio CD of selected poems from this book plus the poet's two earlier volumes published by the University of Arizona Press.

Produced and recorded by Jim Blackwood at the studios of KUAT, Arizona Public Media, on the campus of the University of Arizona, Tucson, Arizona.

track	collection	duration
1. Introduction		0:43
2. Dedication	A Radiant Curve	0:25
3. The beginning was mist	A Radiant Curve	0:24
4. The Canyon Was Serene	A Radiant Curve	4:34
5. Náneeskadí	A Radiant Curve	3:55
6. Far Away	A Radiant Curve	6:22
7. That American Flag	A Radiant Curve	8:21
8. In 1864	Sáanii Dahataał	8:14
9. The warp is even: taut vertical loops	A Radiant Curve	4:33
10. Hills Brothers Coffee	Sáanii Dahataał	2:09
11. Raisin Eyes	Sáanii Dahataał	1:53
12. A Blessing	A Radiant Curve	4:51
13. This Is How They Were Placed for Us	Blue Horses Rush In	7:14
14. Tomorrow I will drive to Shiprock	A Radiant Curve	4:07
15. Tsílii	A Radiant Curve	3:15
16. We must remember	A Radiant Curve	0:28
17. Recording information		0:10

Library of Congress Cataloging-in-Publication Data

Tapahonso, Luci, 1953–

A radiant curve : poems and stories / Luci Tapahonso.

p. cm. — (Sun tracks ; v. 64)

An American Indian literary series

ISBN 978-0-8165-2708-3 (alk. paper) —

ISBN 978-0-8165-2709-0 (pbk. : alk. paper)

1. Navajo Indians—Literary collections. I. Title.

PS3570.A567R33   2008

811'.54—dc22   2008027223